Published in North America by Free Spirit Publishing Inc., Minneapolis, Minnesota, 2017

Library of Congress Cataloging-in-Publication Data
Names: Douglass, Katie, author. | Gordon, Mike, 1948 March 16– illustrator.
Title: Feeling angry! / Katie Douglass ; illustrated by Mike Gordon.
Description: Minneapolis, Minnesota : Free Spirit Publishing, 2017. | Series: Everyday feelings | Audience: Age: 5–9.
Identifiers: LCCN 2017009100| ISBN 9781631982514 (hardback) | ISBN 1631982516 (hardcover)
Subjects: LCSH: Anger in children—Juvenile literature. | CYAC: Anger—Juvenile literature. | BISAC: JUVENILE FICTION /
    Social Issues / Emotions & Feelings. | JUVENILE FICTION / Social Issues / Friendship.
Classification: LCC BF723.A4 D684 2017 | DDC 155.4/1247—dc23 LC record available at https://lccn.loc.gov/2017009100

Reading Level Grade 2; Interest Level Ages 5–9; Fountas & Pinnell Guided Reading Level L

10 9 8 7 6 5 4 3 2 1
Printed in China
H13660517

Free Spirit Publishing Inc.
6325 Sandburg Road, Suite 100
Minneapolis, MN 55427-3674
(612) 338-2068
help4kids@freespirit.com
www.freespirit.com

MIX
Paper from
responsible sources
FSC® C104740

First published in 2017 by Wayland, a division of Hachette Children's Books · London, UK, and Sydney, Australia

Text © Wayland 2017
Illustrations © Mike Gordon 2017

The rights of Katie Douglass to be identified as the author and Mike Gordon as the illustrator of this Work have been asserted in accordance with the Copyright, Designs and Patents Act, 1988.

Managing editor: Victoria Brooker
Creative design: Paul Cherrill

feeling ANGRY!

Written by
Katie Douglass

Illustrated by
Mike Gordon

free spirit
PUBLISHING®

"Aargh, I can't find my bag! Or my keys. And where's my coat?" yelled Harry's dad as he rushed around the kitchen.
Harry's dad was late for work.

AGAIN!

"Dad," said Harry, quietly.
"I've got an idea."
"What is it, Harry?"
his dad snapped angrily.

"You're always telling me not to rush.
If you slow down, maybe that will help?"
suggested Harry.

"Erm, right. Yes, I do say that," Dad said, sheepishly. He stood still, let out a long sigh, and looked around. As he did so, he noticed his coat on the back of a chair. His bag was underneath his coat.

"Look," said Harry. "Your keys are here, too."
Harry's dad smiled. "Thanks, Harry. It's hard to
stay calm when you're in a rush. But now I'd
really better get going! See you tonight."

In the kitchen, Harry's sister, Susie, was asking for a cookie.

"For the third time, *no*, Susie! It's time for breakfast. Now please let me get it ready before I lose my temper," said Susie's mom, sounding very much like she'd already lost her temper.

"But I want a cookie NOW!" Susie shrieked.
Her face was bright red. She looked like
a volcano that had just exploded.

Susie continued to scream.

"Mom, let me try to talk to her," said Harry.

Harry thought that if he could distract Susie, she might stop thinking about cookies.

"Susie, look! It's your favorite TV show."
"Oh, I love this! It's so funny," Susie said,
as she jumped onto the sofa.

Harry breathed a sigh of relief. Now he wouldn't
have to listen to Susie's tantrum anymore.

At school, Harry was on the playground when
two of his friends started fighting.
"Hey!" shouted Lamar. "Give me back the ball!"
"I was playing with it first!" yelled Charlie.

"No you weren't. I was throwing it to Arturo and you just grabbed it. GIVE IT BACK!" Lamar raged.
"NO," replied Charlie, fiercely.
Harry really wanted to play ball, too, but that wasn't going to happen if his friends kept arguing.

"Hey, you two," Harry said.
"We don't have much time left before class.
I don't want to waste it fighting.
Can't we all play together?"

"Hmm, maybe," Charlie grumbled reluctantly.
"I suppose so," mumbled Lamar, looking at his feet.

"Well, what are you waiting for?" called Harry.
"Throw Charlie the ball and let's play!"

In class, Harry's friend Owen was struggling with some math problems. Owen was getting more and more frustrated. Harry could see him tensing his shoulders and clenching his fists.

Finally, Owen snapped. He crumpled
his bit of paper into a ball
and threw it angrily on the floor.
"I can't do it," he ranted.

"Math is hard for me, too," said Harry.
"My mom says, when you're feeling angry,
counting to ten will help you feel better.
Why don't you try that?"

Owen thought this sounded like more math, but he tried it anyway. "1, 2, 3, 4 ...

5, 6, 7...

8, 9, 10."

By the time Owen got to ten, he felt a bit calmer. "It worked!" said Owen, surprised. "I'll ask Ms. Li if she can help us both with this math problem."

That night, Harry was playing on his tablet.
"Time for bed, Harry," his mom called.
"I just need ten more minutes to
finish this game," he pleaded.

"No, Harry. You've already had ten more minutes."

"I haven't," Harry argued, without looking up from his tablet.

"Harry, that's enough. Put the tablet down or you'll have to give it to me."
"That's so unfair!" Harry shouted and stomped off to his room.

"I think maybe it's time he took some of his own advice," said Dad.

Harry was lying face down on his bed, sulking. "Harry," his mom said calmly. "It's time to get ready for bed."

"NO!" shouted Harry angrily.
"Harry, why don't you take some deep
breaths and try to calm down,"
his mom suggested kindly.
"Hmph," growled
Harry, still feeling
annoyed.

"Why don't you slowly count to ten?"
Dad said, peering round the door.
Harry sighed irritably.

Susie appeared. "Hey, Harry.
Come to the bathroom. Mom got you
a new toothbrush!" she said, trying to
distract Harry from his mood.

Harry looked from his mom, to his dad, to his sister and couldn't help but smile. They were all using the advice that he'd been giving out today.

"That's all very good advice," he said.
"And I feel much happier now. But . . .
I still don't want to go to sleep!" and he
started bouncing on the bed.

NOTES FOR PARENTS AND TEACHERS

The aim of this book is to help children think about their feelings in an enjoyable, interactive way. Encourage them to have fun pointing out details in the illustrations, making sound effects, and role playing. Here are more specific ideas for getting the most out of the book:

✴ Encourage children to talk about their own feelings, if they feel comfortable doing so, either while you are reading the book or afterward. Here are a few conversation prompts to try:

- When are some times you feel angry? Why?

- How do you stop feeling angry at those times?

- How do you feel when *other* people are angry?

- This story shows lots of things that people might get angry about, such as difficult schoolwork, rules about bedtime, and not being able to find what you're looking for. What other things can cause us to feel angry? Why do you think different people get angry about different things?

✴ Have children make face masks showing angry expressions. Ask them to explain how these faces show anger.

★ Put on a feelings play! Ask groups of children to act out the different scenarios in the book. They can use their face masks to show when they are angry in the play.

★ Have kids make colorful word clouds. They can start by writing the word *angry,* then add any related words they think of, such as *rage, annoyed,* or *upset.* Have children write their words using different colored pens, making the most important words the biggest and less important words smaller.

★ Invite children to talk about the physical sensations that anger can bring, and where in their bodies they feel anger. Then discuss ways we can calm down when we're angry. Together, practice taking deep breaths and counting to ten.

★ Red is a color that people often connect with anger. Sometimes people even say "I saw red" when they talk about feeling angry. Invite kids to draw red pictures about times when they felt angry. Now, have them draw pictures in another color showing how they dealt with their angry feelings.

For even more ideas to use with this series, download the free Everyday Feelings Leader's Guide at www.freespirit.com/leader.

Note: If a child is continually angry or acts out often due to anger, seek help from a counselor, psychologist, or other health specialist.

BOOKS TO SHARE

A Book of Feelings by Amanda McCardie, illustrated by
Salvatore Rubbino (Walker, 2016)

Cool Down and Work Through Anger by Cheri Meiners,
illustrated by Meredith Johnson (Free Spirit Publishing, 2010)

F Is for Feelings by Goldie Millar and
Lisa A. Berger, illustrated by Hazel Mitchell
(Free Spirit Publishing, 2014)

The Great Big Book of Feelings
by Mary Hoffman, illustrated by Ros Asquith
(Frances Lincoln, 2013)

I Hate Everything! by Sue Graves, illustrated by Desideria Guicciardini
(Free Spirit Publishing, 2014)

Llama Llama Mad at Mama by Anna Dewdney (Viking, 2007)

When I Feel Angry by Cornelia Maude Spelman, illustrated by
Nancy Cote (Albert Whitman & Company, 2000)